Samuel French Acting Edition

I0591740

Seven Spots On The Sun

by Martín Zimmerman

SAMUELFRENCH.COM   SAMUELFRENCH.CO.UK

FOR PRODUCTION ENQUIRIES

UNITED STATES AND CANADA
Info@SamuelFrench.com
1-866-598-8449

UNITED KINGDOM AND EUROPE
Plays@SamuelFrench.co.uk
020-7255-4302

Each title is subject to availability from Samuel French, depending upon country of performance. Please be aware that *SEVEN SPOTS ON THE SUN* may not be licensed by Samuel French in your territory. Professional and amateur producers should contact the nearest Samuel French office or licensing partner to verify availability.

MUSIC USE NOTE

Licensees are solely responsible for obtaining formal written permission from copyright owners to use copyrighted music in the performance of this play and are strongly cautioned to do so. If no such permission is obtained by the licensee, then the licensee must use only original music that the licensee owns and controls. Licensees are solely responsible and liable for all music clearances and shall indemnify the copyright owners of the play(s) and their licensing agent, Samuel French, against any costs, expenses, losses and liabilities arising from the use of music by licensees. Please contact the appropriate music licensing authority in your territory for the rights to any incidental music.

IMPORTANT BILLING AND CREDIT REQUIREMENTS

If you have obtained performance rights to this title, please refer to your licensing agreement for important billing and credit requirements.

SEVEN SPOTS ON THE SUN received its world premiere at Cincinnati Playhouse in the Park in October 2013, directed by KJ Sanchez. The cast was as follows:

MOISÉS...................................... Gerardo Rodriguez
BELÉN .... Ana Grosse
MÓNICA...................................... Gabriela Mayorga
LUIS .... Arturo Soria
TOWN .... Sean Carvajal, Jamie Rezanour, Zuleyma Guevara

CHARACTERS

MOISÉS – Forty-two, a doctor.

BELÉN – Thirty-five, a nurse. Moisés' wife.

EUGENIO – A priest. At least as old as Moisés. Perhaps much older.

MÓNICA – Twenty-seven, a soldier's wife.

LUIS – Thirty-one, Mónica's husband.

TOWN – Three or more – perhaps many more? – men and women. The engine of the play, they portray all roles not named above.

AUTHOR'S NOTES

1. Stage directions in [brackets] indicate movement that is stylized, larger than life, perhaps even choreographed.

2. A stage direction in Roman font indicates a sound that is heightened, more than just representational. When possible, these sounds should be created live by the Town.

3. When an ellipsis appears alone in a line of dialogue it indicates someone struggling to find the right words.

4. When speaking the text in English, actors should use their own natural dialects.

THE TOWN

1. It's *far* more important that you honor the emotional intent of how I have depicted the Town rather than interpret each of the Town's stage directions literally. Feel free to use these stage directions as a blueprint for your work with the Town. Provided, of course, that the story remains clear, and that you preserve the Town's thematic weight, as well as its role as the engine of the play's physical and aural life.

2. *Under no circumstances* should the Town speak all its text in unison. Think of the Town as a drum set. Sometimes all you need is a single snare. At others you will need the tom-tom and bass playing off each other. At others you will need the entire set to get your point across. I have tried to capture this dynamism in how I visually display the Town's text on the page. It is entirely up to you how to divide text between different members of the Town. Make it dynamic. Make it muscular. Make it *physical*.

3. There are two ways the Town can render the parts of the story involving soldados. The first (which will be easier in productions with a smaller Town) is to have the Town physically enact the parts of the story involving soldados as they narrate those parts. The second (which will be easier in productions employing a larger Town) is to have certain members of the Town take on the parts of soldados while other members recount the story.

4. Finally, and perhaps most importantly, the Town should not be a homogenous body of dispassionate observers, but rather a dynamic group of distinct individuals who each have a deeply personal *need* to share this story. To confess, to defend themselves, to enrage you, etc. A single member of the Town can (and probably should) embody a number of these distinct individuals, and each member of the Town should always speak with a *point of view*.

Prologue

(We hear static.)

(*Lights reveal the* **TOWN**.)

(*Everyone hears* the static, *looks at each other...*)

(*At audience...*)

(*Until every single gaze rests on* **EUGENIO**, *who, after some hesitation, steps out from among the* **TOWN**.)

(*The areas of* **EUGENIO**'s *appearance with which he is more fastidious, such as his cuffs and Roman collar, only highlight how disheveled his overall appearance is.*)

EUGENIO. The morning of March fourth?

(*A slight, nervous laugh.*)

(*He feels for his pocket, then, having found it, decides not to remove whatever is in there.*)

I wake up to the sound of static.

(*Lights reveal a radio on a table in the center of the space.*)

TOWN. They'd just repaired the power lines the week before.
So Alamar spent all Saturday looking for a radio.

(**ALAMAR** *steps out from among the* **TOWN**, *approaches the table.*)

A radio to replace the one the army smashed so many months ago.

(**ALAMAR** *watches as* **WILMER** *tinkers with the radio.*)

TOWN. *(With a slight chuckle.)* Only problem was, when they try to hook it up to the speakers...

WILMER. Why isn't it...it's supposed to be...

> (**WILMER** *slaps the radio with his open palm.*)

ALAMAR. ¡Ey!

> (**WILMER** *slaps the radio again.*)

¡Cuidado! ¡Que es un Sony! It's not no cheap piece of shit.

WILMER. Might as well be if we can't get it working...

> (**WILMER** *continues tinkering.* Still static.)

No entiendo... I put the yellow wire in the yellow hole and the red wire in the –

ALAMAR. I thought it would be *so* easy...

WILMER. ¿Y cómo puedo concentrar si tú siempre estás paveando?

ALAMAR. "A genius" you said –

WILMER. Por favor –

ALAMAR. *A genius*...

WILMER. If you hadn't bought a stolen radio...

ALAMAR. *Stolen?*

WILMER. Me escuchaste.

TOWN. All San Isidro is watching waiting for music to pour out of those speakers.

ALAMAR. You have any idea how much I paid for that?

WILMER. Too much.

ALAMAR. Es un Sony, amigo.

WILMER. A stolen Sony.

> (*The* **TOWN** *snickers at* **ALAMAR.**)

ALAMAR. *(Shouting at one of the onlookers.)* Oh, you think it's so funny? *You* come and help.

WILMER. Por favor...

ALAMAR. Think I'm joking? Get over here!

WILMER. They'll just get in the way...

ALAMAR. The way of what? No has hecho nada.

WILMER. If you'll just...give me a minute...

ALAMAR. I gave you two hours!

EUGENIO. Even Moisés is at his door, taking in the morning entertainment.

> *(The light reveals* **MOISÉS** *watching quietly, attentively, apart from the others.)*

WILMER. What you get buying a radio without instructions...

ALAMAR. It came with instructions.

WILMER. I don't speak French.

> *(***ALAMAR*** *tosses* **WILMER** *another set of instructions.)*

ALAMAR. ¿Y coreano?

WILMER. Useless...

> *(And another set of instructions.)*

ALAMAR. Or chino? ¿Hablas chino?

> *(***WILMER*** *shoots him a look.)*

Isn't chino the language of geniuses?

WILMER. Make yourself useful and see if those instructions aren't hiding somewhere.

> *(***ALAMAR*** *searches the box while* **WILMER** *tinkers.)*

ALAMAR. A ver a ver a ver a ver...

> *(And tinkers...)*

...a ver a ver a ver...

> *(...Until the static starts to crackle and we hear faint music.*)*

WILMER. Venga venga venga venga venga...

---

*A license to produce *Seven Spots On The Sun* does not include a performance license for any third-party or copyrighted music. Licensees should create an original composition or use music in the public domain. For further information, please see Music Use Note on page 3.

(**WILMER** *smacks the radio again.*)

ALAMAR. ¡Ey!

(*And again.*)

How many times have I *told* you –

(*One final smack sends Cumbia* spilling out of the speakers.*)

WILMER. ¡Mira!

ALAMAR. How the hell did you...

WILMER. Did I not tell you...?

ALAMAR. Puta madre... Putaputa madre...

WILMER. Did I or didn't I *tell* you –

ALAMAR. You gonna dance with me or what?

(**WILMER** *and* **ALAMAR** *dance with one another.*)

(*Freely, joyfully.*)

(*So freely that they almost forget everyone else, until* **ALAMAR** *remembers the onlookers and shouts:*)

Turn it up! So the whole world can hear!

(*The music nearly swallows the space.*)

[*Everyone spills into la plaza, begins to dance.*]

TOWN. I quickly make up

for eighteen
months
without radio

eighteen months
of daily battle
with my darkest thoughts

---

*A license to produce *Seven Spots On The Sun* does not include a performance license for any third-party or copyrighted music. Licensees should create an original composition or use music in the public domain. For further information, please see Music Use Note on page 3.

> *I* dance
> to *shake* the pain
> out of *every limb*

> to *sweat*
> and sweat
> > till *you've purged* the war
> > from *every pore*

> > > *men* with men
> > > *women* with women

> *eighty-year-olds*
> > *whose* knobby knees
> *stopped* serving them *decades ago*
> > I

> > you

> > > *every one* of us
> > *dance*s!

EUGENIO. Except Moisés.

> (**MOISÉS** *just stands there, watching.*)

> *[While everyone else continues to dance.]*

> *[Feverish.]*

> *[Frenzied.]*

> *[An insatiable appetite for the music.]*

> *[They bathe every part of their body in it.]*

> (*Until a* **VOICE** *crackles in over the radio.*)

VOICE. *We interrupt your regularly scheduled programming...*

> *[Everyone immediately freezes...]*

...for this news break from the capital.

> *[...And stares straight ahead, motionless.]*

The newly-elected gobierno democrático has just passed a landmark piece of legislation pardoning any and all acts of political violence committed during the war.

Presidente Osvaldo Perez is hailing the new amnesty which he promises to sign promptly, as crucial to the maintenance of peace and the continued healing of our country...

(The **VOICE** continues on with a beautiful rhythm and carefully choreographed inflection, but we can't quite make out anything it's saying.)

(After a few moments, we realize it is complete and utter gibberish.)

(Beautiful, but meaningless, gibberish.)

(**MOISÉS** *calmly approaches the radio, gripping a small hammer. Without betraying an ounce of emotion, he begins methodically, mechanically, smashing the radio.*)

(**MOISÉS** *smashes the radio until it's nothing more than a pile of broken plastic pieces.*)

(**EUGENIO** *looks at what's left of the radio, nervously fumbles for his pocket, removes a flask, sips.*)

(*He turns to the audience...*)

EUGENIO. After what the war cost Moisés...no one dares lift a finger to stop him.

One

(**MÓNICA**, *twenty-seven, alone in the space.*)

MÓNICA. I'd just turned twenty.

This was before the war...

He was older. Twenty-four.

He had this...swagger, you know. Was infectious. Like he could look you in the eye, and tell you he was gonna conquer the world, and you'd laugh, 'cause that's what you do when someone says something that stupid, but...you'd still believe it.

Believe *him*.

Least I did.

When he said I was his "missing ingredient."

(*She laughs at that thought.*)

By the time I turn twenty-one we're married. And living in a chozita in Ojona, where Luis is working in the mine on the edge of town.

(*She approaches a wash basin, pulls out a wet garment, starts scrubbing.*)

(**LUIS** *enters from behind, embraces her.*)

LUIS. Why don't you put down that dirty laundry, mi reina, before those smooth hands get all chappy –

MÓNICA. What are you doing here?

LUIS. Uh, I don't get a hello or even like a little smoochy smooch –

MÓNICA. Nope.

LUIS. Why the hell not?

MÓNICA. I could swear it's like three-thirty –

LUIS. Three-fifteen –

MÓNICA. And you're not supposed to get off until –

LUIS. Got off early.

MÓNICA. You got fired.

LUIS. Did I say that, nena?

MÓNICA. They never let anyone off early.

LUIS. Today they did. Let everyone off.
Tunnel collapsed.

MÓNICA. What?!

LUIS. No need to flip a shit. Nobody was even near it, but they shut the whole mine down for safety inspectors or some shit. So I figured I'd come back a bit early...

　　　(Kissing her neck.)

...and sidle up to my sexy lady for some fun –

MÓNICA. They didn't sound the sirens.

LUIS. No one was near it. Happened in some abandoned corridor.

MÓNICA. They're supposed to sound the sirens.

LUIS. Go take it up with the inspector.

MÓNICA. Maybe I will...

LUIS. Mónica –

MÓNICA. What if you were right there when it happened, or it shook the whole mine causing collapse after collapse till mi precioso was swallowed by dust and sweaty rock –

LUIS. *(Pulling away.)* That's a fucking turn off.

MÓNICA. Excuse me?

LUIS. Trying to enjoy a couple extra hours con mi amor and all she can do is spell out apocalyptic equations in her head.

MÓNICA. What can I say? I'm a worrier.

LUIS. No shit.

MÓNICA. Get it from my mother.

LUIS. *(Pulling her up to him.)* Why don't you put your worries in the pocket of those tight little pants so I can strip 'em off your legs and throw 'em out the window as our arms our eyes our skin melt...

(He kisses her.)

(The taste of him turns her on.)

Was thinking about you at work...

MÓNICA. You *were?*

LUIS. When you spend all day blasting at the insides of fertile Mother Earth...

MÓNICA. What were you thinking?

LUIS. Oh, you know...

(Grabbing for her ass.)

...just about those succulent –

MÓNICA. *(Playfully slapping his hand away.)* What else?

LUIS. About what it'll be like when we start to populate this place with our off-growths...

MÓNICA. *(Playful.)* Don't assume.

LUIS. Was thinking we could make a whole equipo de fútbol ourselves.

MÓNICA. How many babies is that?

LUIS. How many times you watch me play fútbol, nena?

MÓNICA. Don't know. Lots.

LUIS. How many guys you see running around out there?

MÓNICA. Wasn't counting.

LUIS. Eleven on a side.

MÓNICA. Eleven?

LUIS. And a couple more if we wanna have some substitutes.

MÓNICA. *Eleven?*

LUIS. But you know what? We're not gonna have any substitutes. Our babies are gonna be strong, potros salvajes running around that pitch.

MÓNICA. I'm gonna get all stretched out!

LUIS. Never!

MÓNICA. Promise?

LUIS. I swear.

MÓNICA. *(Grabbing him.)* When do we get started?

LUIS. Not quite yet, negra.

MÓNICA. Why not?

LUIS. *(Playful.)* I gotta surprise for you...

MÓNICA. What is it?

LUIS. A lavadora.

MÓNICA. You serious?!

LUIS. I'm talkin' six-speeds state of the art spin cycle and everything –

MÓNICA. Ohmygodohmygodohmygod!

LUIS. Mi reina's never washing anything with her bare hands again...

> *(Kissing her neck.)*

Her hands will stay smooth for all eternity, just like her lips...

MÓNICA. How'd you pay for a washer?

> *(He looks at her, smiles.)*

LUIS. Mónica, Mónica, Mónica...

MÓNICA. What?

LUIS. Why you gotta be so...

MÓNICA. *What?*

LUIS. I come home with good news, somethin' to celebrate, and all you can do is –

MÓNICA. You won't tell me, will you?

LUIS. That's not what I'm... Did I say I wouldn't –

MÓNICA. Then say it.

How'd you pay for a washer?

> *(Brief pause.)*

LUIS. They promoted me.

> *(She looks at him.)*

MÓNICA. Mentiroso.

LUIS. Mónica –

MÓNICA. You're lying.

LUIS. You know how many women would just be grateful to have a dedicated husband who stops at nothing to bring them a better life –

MÓNICA. I'm not just any woman.

LUIS. Right about that, negra. Any other woman would wrap her arms around this proveedor, squeeze his ass, and celebrate like we're s'posed to. But not my Mónica. *No.* My woman's gotta be the one woman in the *world* who spoils the moment askin' all these *questions* –

MÓNICA. You don't like it? Leave.

> *(Brief pause.)*

LUIS. Mónica…

MÓNICA. If your life would be so much better with all these other women –

LUIS. That's not what I'm sayin' –

MÓNICA. Door's open.

> *(No answer.)*

How'd you pay for a washer?

> *(Pause. He takes out a piece of paper, hands it over.)*

There wasn't a tunnel collapse, was there?

> *(No answer.)*

Thought we talked about this.

LUIS. A man's not entitled to change his mind?

MÓNICA. *Luis* –

LUIS. Oh no no no no no, don't you go saying my name like that –

MÓNICA. You know this makes me nervous. My –

LUIS & MÓNICA. – Uncle –

LUIS. – I know –

MÓNICA. Sits in a corner staring into space all day.

LUIS. Well, maybe that's the result of his smoking *marijuana* all day for twenty-two years.

(**MÓNICA** *looks at him.*)

LUIS. Got tired of that prick manager riding my ass.

MÓNICA. So you trade a prick manager riding your ass for some prick sargento?

LUIS. That's just the first few months, nena. When basic's over, I just sit around playing cards with a rifle slung over my back.

(*No answer.*)

What's the worst that could happen?

MÓNICA. Oh, I don't know, you could get *killed*?

LUIS. When?

MÓNICA. Oh, I don't know, in a *war*?

LUIS. With who?

(*No answer.*)

Our next-door neighbors?

MÓNICA. I don't know, I don't know...

LUIS. You ever been across the border? Talked to those people?

(*No answer.*)

I have. Drank vino with them, smoked some *marijuana* with them, and I'll tell you what, nena, those people are about as interested in fighting as I am in getting my prick pierced. So what are you so worried about?

(*Taking her in his arms.*)

I'm gonna put my time in, never work a day in that mine again, and I'm gonna come out with a big fat pension –

MÓNICA. How fat?

LUIS. Fatter than your Aunt Nilda's thighs.

MÓNICA. That's *fat*...

LUIS. And we're gonna use it to buy a little house with all the aparatos we need, so we won't have to worry about anything other than staying strong and sexy and churning out our little futbolistas. And we'll sit outside sipping some vino every night, and call ourselves Saavedra United.

MÓNICA. What if we fight ourselves?

LUIS. Ourselves?

MÓNICA. When I was at the mercado Adriana was saying how on the radio they keep talking about some retired general who says he's not gonna sit around and watch the PPR win an election –

LUIS. So now you listen to every last chismosa like she's spouting gospel truth?

MÓNICA. Baby –

LUIS. That's funny.

MÓNICA. Luis –

LUIS. No, I'm serious, nena. You are a Grade A comedian.

*(**LUIS** kisses her, vanishes.)*

MÓNICA. Next weekend he's off to basic.

And works his way up quick. All the way to Sargento by the end of the year.

When the junta deposes the PPR government.

And the war begins.

Two

EUGENIO. The war has just turned three.

> (*The faint glow of artillery emanates from the horizon.*)

TOWN. The civil war our town knows too well.
> No sooner does one side take us
> than *we slip* through their grasp.
>> *Both sides* take to
>> calling us *La
>> Resbalosa.*

Because we're so hard to hold.
> You grow used
> to the sound of *shells
> singing you to sleep.*

(We hear the whirr of distant shells.)

EUGENIO. Thank God we have Moisés...
And Belén beside him...

> (**MOISÉS** *enters, his doctor's coat covered in blood.*)

> (**BELÉN** *trails behind, shell-shocked, as* **MOISÉS** *removes his coat, scrubs his hands clean...*)

TOWN. *I* watch them tirelessly treat
each inocente
that comes to their clinic
> each bystander
> caught in the crossfire
>> you watch them heal
>> every wound imaginable

all without losing a step.
> Well maybe Moisés doesn't
> But Belén...

> (**MOISÉS** *approaches the stunned* **BELÉN**, *tries to hold her, comfort her...*)

(But she shrinks away from his touch.)

TOWN. The war seems to cost her more than most.
And Belén
she has more life
more fire than almost anyone
So when it starts to go out
When she stops giggling
each time she hears your baby's heartbeat
Stops smiling as she welcomes you into the clinic...
We notice
How could we not?

EUGENIO. Yet they still forge ahead.
Do what they must.
So I do all I can to help them
make sure they have supplies.
Even ride with Moisés to Pilar
tell the soldados we're on official Church business
to get him through the checkpoints.

> *(**MOISÉS** sits in a chair, "drives.")*
>
> *(**EUGENIO** sits next to him.)*

I forge elaborate letters
and when some soldado
asks too many questions
or wants a bigger bribe than we can give
I look him in the eye and say
"The Bishop will not be pleased."

> *(**EUGENIO** holds a stern gaze...)*
>
> *(Then cracks a wide smile.)*

Works like a charm.

> *(**EUGENIO** laughs out loud.)*

MOISÉS. They teach you that stunt in the seminary? Or is that a Padre Eugenio original?

EUGENIO. Stunt?

MOISÉS. The Dirty Harry bit.

One of these days you're gonna try it and they're gonna call your bluff, blow both our heads off.

EUGENIO. Not with God's hand guiding us.

MOISÉS. Since when was God in the business of forging letters? I thought he had more urgent matters to attend to.

EUGENIO. He is in everything.

MOISÉS. Is he in the shrapnel that shredded that kid's leg?

(*No answer.*)

One of these days I'm gonna get you to admit I'm right. That you're too smart to believe all this nonsense.

EUGENIO. That doesn't strike you as hypocritical? To mock my faith but still use it when it suits you?

(**MOISÉS** *looks at him.*)

Maybe you should try your next supply run without me. See how many checkpoints you make it through.

(**MOISÉS** *smiles. Point taken.*)

EUGENIO. Through our...arrangement

we manage to spare San Isidro the worst of it

to take the edge off this war.

(**MOISÉS** *vanishes.*)

TOWN. Until May of that third year.

When Presidente Alvarez decides to end the war before the upcoming elections.

End the war on his own terms.

(*The distant glow burns closer, brighter.*)

(The whirr of the shells grows more intense.)

The army spares nothing
in their freshest assault.

                    They sweep through the town
*cut*ting all *the power* lines
            *smash*ing *every radio* in sight

and when the PPR guerrilleros
try to take it back

the fighting is fierce.

*(The sound of the shells builds and builds to
a frenzy until...)*

(Silence.)

But this time when the smoke clears

the winning side

doesn't leave a severed head

or arm

as a sign of their commitment

to the cause...

EUGENIO. This time the Sargento ups the ante.

*[The silhouette of the Sargento appears on a
scrim.]*

*[**SOLDADOS** drag a **YOUNG MAN** through the
street.]*

*(We hear the scraping sound of the **YOUNG
MAN**'s body dragging across the gravel road.)*

*(The **YOUNG MAN** moans with every single
scrape.)*

TOWN. The *soldados drag* a boy of about fifteen
                a PPR guerrillero

or so they say

they leave him in la plaza
                broken

                        bleeding

                                clinging to life.

*[A **SOLDADO** enters with a wooden plank and
a can of paint.]*

Then they
stick a wooden plank
in the ground

TOWN. beside his body...

> [The **SOLDADO** *slams the plank in the ground...*]

...crack a can of paint...

> [*Opens the can of paint...*]

...dip their palms in it
and each one
leaves his mark.

> [*...And leaves a white palm print on the wooden plank.*]

Then they leave.
On to the next town.

> (*The* **SOLDADO** *vanishes.*)

> [*The* **YOUNG MAN** *continues clinging to life.*]

> (*As* **MOISÉS** *and* **BELÉN** *watch from their window.*)

MOISÉS. It's a loyalty test.

BELÉN. It's a challenge.
They're telling us if we leave him there we're the same as them.

MOISÉS. Is that what they're telling us? Or what you're thinking?

> (*No answer.*)

We'll never be the same as them.

BELÉN. The second you say that is the second we start to become them.

MOISÉS. Belén –

BELÉN. We have to help him, prove them wrong.

MOISÉS. And what happens when they come back? What happens to everyone who comes to the clinic for our help after they've killed us?

> (*No answer.*)

I hate it every bit as much as you do, Belén. But we
have to learn to live with this one.

> (*She says nothing.*)

EUGENIO. I sit at my window
staring at the boy
recalling whispers
of nuns in other towns
who dared
step in the fray.
Nuns who were raped
and left for dead.
I wonder if it's worth the risk.

> (*A knock.*)

> (**MOISÉS** *appears.*)

MOISÉS. I'm low, need to make another run.

> (*Silence.*)

You coming?

> (*Brief pause.* **EUGENIO** *nods.*)

> (**MOISÉS** *sits in a chair, "drives," as* **EUGENIO**
> *continues to address the audience.*)

> (*All the while, the* **YOUNG MAN** *clings to life
> across the space.*)

EUGENIO. The entire trip
to Pilar
and back
I'm hoping he'll
say something
give some sign...

> (**MOISÉS** *stares straight ahead.*)

But when we return
see the boy
still struggling

EUGENIO. Moisés just lets me off...

>   (**MOISÉS** *and* **EUGENIO** *look at each other.*)

...gives his customary...

MOISÉS. Gracias.

EUGENIO. ...And drives away.

>   (**MOISÉS** *exits.*)

I return to the window
and watch the boy
disappear in the darkness.

>   (*Lights slowly fade on the* **YOUNG MAN.**)

TOWN. What do we do?
What can we do?
I'm not a doctor. Are you?
We can still do something.
He's just a boy.
Give him some water, say a prayer...
No older than my son.
Doesn't make him an inocente.
Not much, but it's something.
At what cost?
Inocente or not. He's still just a...
You go first.

>   (*No one moves.*)

EUGENIO. I fall asleep. To escape my doubts.

>   (**EUGENIO** *exits.*)
>
>   (*Lights rise on* **BELÉN** *at home, anxiously preparing the table for a meal.*)
>
>   (**MOISÉS** *enters, takes his pack off.* **BELÉN** *immediately rushes to him, embraces him.*)
>
>   (*He holds her close.*)

BELÉN. You said Three.

MOISÉS. They doubled the number of checkpoints. Takes forever to get nowhere.

BELÉN. Already did.

MOISÉS. Now it takes twice as forever.

> *(She kisses him, goes for the pack.)*

BELÉN. What did you...?

> *(**MOISÉS** pulls the pack away before she can get to it, begins emptying it.)*

MOISÉS. Extra gauze...iodine...

BELÉN. Good...

MOISÉS. Lost most of the morphine on the way back...

BELÉN. You serious?

MOISÉS. Every son of a bitch soldado between here and Pilar wanted to skim some off the top.

BELÉN. You didn't bribe them with booze?

MOISÉS. They wanted morphine. I wasn't about to argue.

> *(He looks at her.)*

> *(She takes his head in her hands, kisses him.)*

No one else needs treatment?

> *(No answer.)*

¿Belén?

BELÉN. *(Pulling away.)* No sé.

MOISÉS. Did anyone come to the clinic?

> *(She shakes her head.)*

MOISÉS. Then no one else needs –

BELÉN. What about...?

> *(No answer.)*

He still out there?

> *(No answer.)*

It's been quiet.

MOISÉS. Don't worry about it.

BELÉN. *Him.*

MOISÉS. No te preocupes.

(She stares at him.)

MOISÉS. There's nothing to be done.

> *(No answer.)*
>
> *(He kisses her forehead, embraces her, sways with her in silence.)*
>
> *(As they sway, a big, boyish smile finds its way onto his face.)*

BELÉN. Moisés, please, I'm not in the mood.

MOISÉS. Sometimes we must summon the mood.

> *(Beat.)*

Cierra los ojos.

BELÉN. What are you up to?

MOISÉS. Close your eyes and you'll find out.

BELÉN. You know I don't like –

MOISÉS. This will be worth it.

> *(She obliges.)*
>
> *(He pulls a piña [pineapple] out of the pack.)*

Abre.

> *(She opens her eyes.)*

BELÉN. *Por Dios...*

MOISÉS. I dare you
to find someone
who can honestly say
they've seen
a more perfect piña.

BELÉN. It's been...

MOISÉS. I know...

BELÉN. *Years...*

> *(He delicately places the piña in her hands. She admires it.)*

MOISÉS. I was leaving the Red Cross clinic when I saw an army truck filled to the top with them. Apparently, one of the comandantes has an appetite...

*(**BELÉN**'s face immediately falls.)*

...and ordered a private shipment –

BELÉN. What did it cost you?

MOISÉS. *(With a laugh.)* Cost me?

BELÉN. You didn't steal it, did you?

MOISÉS. Claro que no, I –

BELÉN. What did it cost you?

(No answer.)

*(**BELÉN** stares at the piña in her hands, laughs a single, harsh laugh.)*

You mean, we could've had all our morphine if you hadn't –

MOISÉS. We'll be fine.

BELÉN. If we aren't? If we run out?

MOISÉS. I'll get more.

BELÉN. If the roads are blocked?

MOISÉS. Belén –

BELÉN. Or Padre Eugenio can't go with you? Or –

MOISÉS. We don't need morphine.

BELÉN. We need this?

(Beat.)

MOISÉS. Soon as I saw those piñas
    piled in the back of that truck
    I knew I was bringing one home to you.
    I didn't care what it would cost.
    If he'd asked for my foot
    I'd have gladly cut it off –

BELÉN. Amor, don't say that...

MOISÉS. Would've given it up in an instant
    for the chance to bring this back
    and hear that laugh...

BELÉN. Don't know what you're talking about...

MOISÉS. The laugh that opened the eyes of a shy, bookish
    boy...

(Taking her in his arms.)

MOISÉS. ...who walked around
wearing a stern look on his face
because he was searching
so desperately
for the one thought
that would shift
how he understood everything.
Only he imagined this thought
was way up in the ether
tip-toeing across the clouds.
Until he met a *woman*...

*(He looks at **BELÉN**.)*

BELÉN. Who looked him in the eye...

MOISÉS. And said...

BELÉN. Have you ever noticed
how piña
starts to burn
if you hold
it on your tongue
too long?

MOISÉS. And the boy
could honestly say
it was a thought
he'd never had.
Even though he'd spent
his whole life
thinking
and eating piña...

BELÉN. So I sliced off a piece...

MOISÉS. Slipped it in my mouth...

BELÉN. Threw my head back...

MOISÉS. And laughed larger
than any woman

I'd ever seen
laughed the laugh
of a man
three times
your size
and I loved it.

> *(She pulls a knife out of her apron and is about to sink it into the piña, when...)*

> *(A single scream.)*

> *(She looks at* **MOISÉS**.*)*

Nothing to be done.

> *(Another scream.)*

> *(She looks at* **MOISÉS**.*)*

> *(She plunges the knife into the piña, cuts out a piece, hands it to him.)*

> *(He bites into it, makes a noise as soon as he does.)*

> *(She looks at him, expectant.)*

Sabrosísima...

> *(She cuts out a piece of her own, takes a bite.)*

> *(Then another. And another.)*

Not so fast –

> *(And another.)*

> *(And another.)*

You have to savor –

> *(She continues biting ravenously, panicked, until tears stream down her face.)*

¿Belén...?

BELÉN. They've done it...they've finally, finally –

MOISÉS. Done...?

BELÉN. Chipped away
at me

bit by bit
and I just sat there
let them
didn't even
put up a fight –

MOISÉS. ¿Qué dices? –

BELÉN. Every time
they left a corpse
en la plaza
tied an enemy
to the back of their truck
and laid on the gas
every time
I told my
my tongue
my eyes
my nose
my ears
not to
taste
see
smell
hear
what was right
in front of them
and finally
they've started to obey.

MOISÉS. You mean...

BELÉN. It started
with my eyes
colors bleeding
into each other
till I couldn't tell
them apart
then sounds

started feeling
farther
and farther
away –

MOISÉS. You never said anything.

BELÉN. I thought
maybe my mind
was playing tricks
que me estaba
engañando
but now
I know.

> *(Silence.)*

I can't even feel the burning on my tongue.

> *(Pause.)*

MOISÉS. *(Picking up the piña)* We'll save it for later.

BELÉN. You're not listening –

MOISÉS. For when you're feeling better –

BELÉN. It won't change a thing.

> *(Another scream.)*
>
> *(She looks at* **MOISÉS**.*)*

MOISÉS. Even if he could be saved...

BELÉN. He's lived this long.

MOISÉS. They'll be back. To collect a corpse. Along with anyone who's laid a finger on him.

BELÉN. It's after dark. The power's out –

MOISÉS. Doesn't make a difference –

BELÉN. We nurse him to health, let him go back to the PPR, no one will know –

MOISÉS. Everyone will.

BELÉN. Then they fucking know.
But at least
I can feel

my lover's skin
against my own.

> *(She kisses him, fully, aggressively, as if trying to feel something, anything.)*
>
> *(She pulls her head away, stares at him.)*
>
> *(Silence.)*

MOISÉS. We go get him together.
You can't carry him alone.

> *(He follows her off.)*
>
> *(**EUGENIO** appears.)*

EUGENIO. The next morning I wake
and go straight to the window...

> *(The **TOWN** appears around the edges of the space, staring at the empty space where the young man lay.)*

TOWN. Is he dead?

EUGENIO. But all I see...

TOWN. Alive?

EUGENIO. ...Are the milky palm prints...

TOWN. Did someone try to treat him?

EUGENIO. ...On that wooden plank.

TOWN. Bury his body?

EUGENIO. And when Moisés passes me in the street...

> *(**MOISÉS** enters, en route to somewhere else.)*

He walks away
before I can open my mouth.

> *(**MOISÉS** glances at **EUGENIO** momentarily, but quickly walks away, disappears.)*

Three

(The sound of banging on metal invades the space.)

TOWN. Within a week
the soldados return.

[*The* TOWN *appears around the edges of the space, stomping rhythmically on sheets of corrugated tin.*]

From my window

I

You

see the Sargento
get out of his truck
carrying a can of paint
and *lead his men*
around the corner.

[*The Sargento's silhouette walks across the scrim. The can of paint swings in his hand as he disappears.*]

[*The* TOWN *continues to stomp as...*]

(*Lights reveal* BELÉN *cleaning medical instruments in the clinic. After a moment,* MOISÉS *enters.*)

BELÉN. How far?

MOISÉS. Five houses from the corner. Or four.

BELÉN. You couldn't tell?

MOISÉS. Didn't want to risk them spotting me while I spied from the roof.

EUGENIO. I can only listen
as the soldados knock...

[*The* TOWN *stomps in unison.*]

...on the door...

      [Stomp.]

EUGENIO. ...after door...

      [Stomp.]

  ...looking for what they left behind.

BELÉN. Fifteen houses from us.

MOISÉS. How do you figure?

BELÉN. They work their way down the other side of the street, then around –

MOISÉS. They'll criss-cross.

      (Beat.)

  Ten away. At most.

TOWN. Each knock

          brings a pair

              of eager eyes

     to the window

                    where I *watch*

                you *wonder*

         we *wait.*

    [With each successive stomp, another member of the TOWN raises a frame to their face and peers through it at the center of the space.]

BELÉN. If we hadn't waited. If we'd gone out there and grabbed him right away –

MOISÉS. Belén –

BELÉN. – We could've nursed him to health – been done with this – days ago –

MOISÉS. But we didn't.

      (Silence. He embraces her.)

BELÉN. ¿Pues qué hacemos?

MOISÉS. We hide him in the house.

BELÉN. Where?

MOISÉS. We'll find somewhere.

BELÉN. He's delirious. He'll start screaming soon as they come in.

MOISÉS. It's a risk we have to take.

BELÉN. Not if we take him.

(**BELÉN** *looks at him.*)

MOISÉS. We've been over this. We decided –

BELÉN. *You* did.

MOISÉS. Belén –

BELÉN. Our chances are so much better inside that church...

MOISÉS. It's cement walls. Not some magic sanctuary.

BELÉN. ...So much better than our chances in the house.

MOISÉS. If Eugenio lets us in.

BELÉN. Why wouldn't he?

(*No answer.*)

Why is it so hard for you to trust him?

MOISÉS. Why isn't it harder for you?

BELÉN. Just because the man wears a Roman collar doesn't mean –

MOISÉS. He only acts the way he does because he believes some imaginary friend is peeking over his shoulder taking notes. Not because he has any conviction that what he's doing is wrong or right –

BELÉN. I don't see how that makes any difference.

MOISÉS. It makes all the difference.

BELÉN. He'll still do it, just the same.

(*No answer.*)

How many times has he risked his life with you?

[Stomp.]

(**MOISÉS** *and* **BELÉN** *look at each other. They vanish.*)

TOWN. The clinic door opens.

(**MOISÉS** *and* **BELÉN** *enter, carrying a covered stretcher.*)

TOWN. Moisés and Belén emerge
  carrying the boy across the street.
EUGENIO. I'm in such a state of shock
  it's not until they pound...

    [Stomp.]

...on my door
that I realize
they've come to me
that this is my chance
to do what I should have done
days ago
stand up
in the face of this
insanity
and all I have to do
is open a door...

    [The **TOWN** *is silent, still, watching through
    their frames.]*

In my mind
I see myself
usher them into the sacristy
and tell them to stay silent
as the Sargento
pounds on the door
demands I let him in
I see myself
give him the same icy stare
I gave so many soldados
before him
and watch him
walk away
I can see it all
clear as day
but as I lay my hand

on the latch...

(**EUGENIO** *reaches his hand out.*)

...the Sargento
comes round the corner
can of paint
swinging
in his hand.

[We see the Sargento's silhouette.]

[And hear the can of paint creaking as it swings in his hand.]

He's framed
in the space between
Belén's shoulder
and the edge of the window
growing
ever so slowly
as he approaches...

[The Sargento slowly grows.]

Pero en ese momento
as I try to open the latch
mis manos me traizionan
mis piernas
y mis pies
my whole body
betrays me
as I bolt the door
and walk away...

(*A wave of panic washes over* **MOISÉS** *and* **BELÉN.**)

[They pound on the door and scream.]

[The Sargento continues to grow on the scrim behind them.]

...as my feet

carry me into the sacristy
and I barricade
myself inside it.
But I can't escape
the sound of their screams
so I tear the pockets
out of my pants
stuff the cotton in my ears
and when that doesn't stop
the echoing
I see...

> *(A large decanter of sacramental wine appears.)*
>
> *(**EUGENIO** picks it up.)*
>
> *[He chugs and chugs the wine.]*
>
> *[The Sargento grows and grows.]*
>
> *[The **TOWN** tries to look away, but can't.]*
>
> *[**MOISÉS** and **BELÉN** pound the door.]*
>
> *[The Sargento grows until he envelops the screen in black.]*
>
> *(**MOISÉS** and **BELÉN** vanish.)*
>
> *[**EUGENIO**, having finished the decanter in a single gulp, collapses on the floor.]*

(Slowly pulling himself off the ground.) The next morning
I stumble onto the street
to see a smattering
of milky palm prints
staring at me
from the clinic door.

> *(A **SOLDADO** enters, dips his hand in the can of paint, smacks his print on the tin door.)*
>
> *(The **TOWN** holds the door up so **EUGENIO** can see.)*

Four

(**MÓNICA**, *alone in the space.*)

MÓNICA. Once the war starts
Luis is five weeks in the field
one week at home
five weeks in the field
one week at home...
At first it's fine.
Great, even.
For five weeks
at a time
we store up our anxiety
our *deseos sexuales*
wrap them into tight little balls of energía
and soon as he steps through the door
we unleash them on each other
for seven days straight.
Neither of us gets more than five feet from the bed
before a sweaty hand
or quivering leg
pulls us into orbit.
Milk spoils
bread rots
fruit draws flies
we sustain *each other...*

(**LUIS** *steps into the space in his fatigues, a duffle bag slung over one shoulder and his right hand in his pocket.*)

(**MÓNICA** *stares at him for a moment, lost.*)

(*Then she runs at him, leaps into his arms.*)

(*At the moment of contact, he comes to life, catches her.*)

How've you been, baby?

LUIS. Was a lot better before you started strangling me.

MÓNICA. Excuse me?

LUIS. Feel like my windpipe's blocked up –

MÓNICA. *(Kissing him all over.)* I thought crawling through the selva all day, thought cutting through the viñas con tu machete, thought all that hard labor was supposed to make you stronger –

LUIS. Maybe you got heavier.

> *(She lets go of him, backs away.)*

MÓNICA. Well, fuck you, too.

LUIS. I didn't... You know I didn't mean that –

MÓNICA. You said it.

LUIS. Yeah, but I didn't... I uh...

> *(Pulling something out of his duffle bag.)*

...got you a gift.

> *(He tosses her a bag of M&M's.)*

MÓNICA. This wrapper's in –

LUIS. English.

MÓNICA. Wait, how did you –

LUIS. There's a gringo officer who's been following us in the field.

MÓNICA. Following you?

LUIS. Keeping us in line. Teaching us all his tried and true gringo tactics so we can get the best of the hijos de puta in the PPR, you know?

MÓNICA. Maybe.

LUIS. He's always telling us we get too antsy in the field.

> *(Imitating a gringo accent.)*

"That's the problem with you Hispanics. Living so close to the equator makes your blood boil too easy." Says it just like that. Just like John Wayne. And he gives us these golocinas, tells us to suck on something sweet, to keep us calm in the field, while we wait –

MÓNICA. So you're saying if I suck on these while you're away, the next five weeks will fly by –

LUIS. I just...thought you'd want something sweet.

MÓNICA. I do...

> *(She kisses him softly, sweetly, then tries to move into something more. He pulls away.)*

¿Qué pasa? You don't want to –

LUIS. I do, I do, I just –

MÓNICA. What?

> *(No answer.)*

You got another gift for me?

LUIS. Huh?

MÓNICA. Don't think I haven't noticed.

LUIS. Don't know what you're talking about –

MÓNICA. Your right hand hasn't left your pocket since you stepped inside, baby. You must be hiding something special –

LUIS. There's really...there's nothing –

MÓNICA. *(Reaching for his hand.)* I caught you, mi vida. Found you out. Might as well give up the game.

LUIS. There's nothing in there, Mónica –

MÓNICA. *(In a playful, pleading voice.)* Por favor, mi amor...

LUIS. I told you to –

> *(She grabs at his hand.)*
>
> *(He throws her off himself with both hands.)*

– stay away!

> *(We see his hand exposed in the light.)*
>
> *(The top half of his right ring finger is missing. Silence.)*

MÓNICA. What the hell happened?

LUIS. It's none of your business.

MÓNICA. What do you mean it's none of my business? Half your fucking finger is –

LUIS. It's nothing you need to worry about.

MÓNICA. Were you thinking I wouldn't notice?

LUIS. I knew it –

MÓNICA. Thinking you'd walk around all week with your hand in your pocket and I'd never notice –

LUIS. Knew you'd react this way

MÓNICA. What way?

LUIS. *Lo sabía* –

MÓNICA. What way Luis?

LUIS. I knew you wouldn't understand.

MÓNICA. Understand? There's nothing about it to understand, mi vida, I'm upset you got your finger blown off is all, I'm upset at the situation is all, baby, but I wasn't suggesting this was your...

(He looks at her.)

Are you...are you saying that you –

LUIS. It didn't get blown off is what I'm saying.

MÓNICA. Then what...what...

LUIS. Got run over. By an APC and...it's kinda hard to explain how it happened, but long story short it got smashed real bad and...the medic wanted to treat it, let it heal right, but that would've meant more than a month out of the field and...

MÓNICA. So you...

LUIS. Held my knife over a hot flame, sliced it off myself.

(Silence.)

Would've meant more than a month out of the field –

MÓNICA. A month at home with me, helping you heal –

LUIS. Told you, you wouldn't understand.

MÓNICA. You're right. I don't understand.

LUIS. They're *my* men. *My* responsibility. I wasn't about to abandon them. Not after what we...

MÓNICA. What you...?

LUIS. It's just a fucking finger.

MÓNICA. *Your* finger. A part of mi amor. And you just... threw it away –

LUIS. Sorry I even brought it up, sorry I even tried to be honest with you – can we just...

> *(He kisses her. As if to initiate sex.)*
>
> *(But it's clear he's read the situation wrong.)*
>
> *(She pulls away.)*

What's the matter?

You were the one who was all over me soon as I stepped through the door.

MÓNICA. I'm just feeling a little um...a little –

LUIS. What?

> *(Grabbing hold of her.)*

Come on, baby. Let's have some fun.

MÓNICA. Don't, Luis –

LUIS. ¿No te la como todita, mamita?

MÓNICA. Please –

LUIS. What's the matter? You don't like dirty talk?

MÓNICA. Luis –

LUIS. You always like a little dirty talk –

MÓNICA. *(Violently throwing him off.)* Get the fuck OFF!

> *(Beat.)*

LUIS. You're so fucking ungrateful, you know that? *Ingrata.* Here I am, putting my life on the line every day to buy you a better place in this world, to make sure some punk-ass PPR guerrilleros don't gun you down in your home and you look at me like...just like all these peasants, all these *indios* look at us every time we comb through their towns, I just want to smack 'em on the head and be like, "Coño, we are doing this for *you*. To *protect* you," but all they can do is look at us like we're monsters, me estas mirando como si fuera mónstruo, Mónica, and it's so fucking... It's fucking...

(Tears stream down his face.)

MÓNICA. You alright, mi vida?

LUIS. I'm fine, I'm fine –

MÓNICA. You're crying.

LUIS. I'm not.

MÓNICA. *(Taking him into her lap.)* Shhh...

LUIS. I'm not crying.

MÓNICA. Why don't you just rest...

LUIS. Your hands...

MÓNICA. What about them?

LUIS. Have you been using the...washer?

MÓNICA. Of course, mi vida.

LUIS. No, you haven't.

MÓNICA. Maybe sometimes I like to wash with my hands, maybe just to keep my mind off other things –

LUIS. Promise you'll use it always.

MÓNICA. Of course. I promise.

LUIS. *(Drifting off to sleep.)* And when my big fat pension comes, fatter than your Aunt Nilda's thighs, we'll buy ourselves a little house with all the aparatos we need...

(She caresses his hair, turns to the audience.)

MÓNICA. Each time after that
his body comes back to me
but...it's like he's leaving little bits of himself
in the field
an earlobe here
a pinky toe there
so when the war ends... I barely have a husband.
So I have to carve a child – our Ailén – out of the two of us myself.
And pray she can resurrect him.
A week after the war ends, the army lets him go. Says he's not fit for service, because, well, he's not, and since he only served four years...we can kiss that pension goodbye.

Luis tries going back to the mine, but even they won't take him, and...

(She can't help but laugh.)

...a month later our lavadora breaks.

I try to have it hauled out of here, see if we can sell it for scrap, but Luis...for the first time in months, he looks me in the eye, begs me to keep it.

Five

(**EUGENIO** *and the* **TOWN** *in the empty space.*)

TOWN.   After the soldados take Belén
Moisés disappears from sight
making only the occasional trip out
             for food or water.
                        He doesn't dare set foot in the clinic.
             The war ends a month later.

EUGENIO. The few times I pass him in the street
I don't have the heart
to look in his direction.

> (**EUGENIO** *feels for his pocket, pulls out his flask, sips.*)

TOWN. Until eighteen months after the end of the war...
The day radio returned to San Isidro...

> (*We hear faint echoes of the beautiful Cumbia music.**)
>
> [*Everyone dances.*]

The day they passed the Amnesty...

> (*The music is interrupted by* the indecipherable gibberish of the radio announcer.)
>
> [*Everyone stares straight ahead, mouths agape.*]

EUGENIO. The day Moisés smashed Alamar's radio.

> (**MOISÉS** *appears.*)
>
> (The sound of smashing *as he swings his hammer at the empty air over and over.*)
>
> (**EUGENIO** *and the* **TOWN** *vanish.*)

---

*A license to produce *Seven Spots On The Sun* does not include a performance license for any third-party or copyrighted music. Licensees should create an original composition or use music in the public domain. For further information, please see Music Use Note on page 3.

(**MOISÉS** *tosses the hammer aside, enters his home, which is barren except for...*)

(*A massive pile of piñas.*)

(**MOISÉS** *picks one out of the pile, cuts a chunk out of it, bites into the flesh, then promptly tosses it aside.*)

(*He repeats this process with another piña.*)

(*And another.*)

(*Until* **BELÉN** *appears.*)

BELÉN. You gonna save some for me?

MOISÉS. Is that really you...?

> [*She laughs the laugh of a man three times her size.*]

Claro...

> (*But as soon as he sees her,* **MOISÉS** *starts to weep.*)

BELÉN. ¿Por qué estás llorando, amor?

MOISÉS. Perdóname, mi vida...

BELÉN. For what?

MOISÉS. I failed you.

BELÉN. You didn't –

MOISÉS. I let the soldados take you from me and now I'll never get you back.

BELÉN. ¿Qué dices?

MOISÉS. You didn't hear what they said on the radio?
Amnesty...
Who knew one hateful word can do so much damage.
Amnesty...
"For the continued healing of our country," they said.
But how can I heal when they'll never tell me where you are
never return you to me
so I can lay you to rest

in some soft patch of earth
where I can sit by your side
while the breeze whispers tonterías in our ears.

BELÉN. And this is why the piñas.

MOISÉS. When I was breaking that radio to bits
a cold clarity came over me
una convicción
that this was the only way left
to keep you alive in my mind.
Packing my possessions
all the useless debris
de mi vida sin tí
piling it in our truck
to barter it all away
in search of a piña whose taste
can match the one
you slipped in my mouth so many years ago...

BELÉN. And it worked! I'm here!

MOISÉS. I can already
feel you flickering
fading...

> *[**BELÉN** flickers before our eyes.]*

BELÉN. Maybe you haven't found the right one...

> *(**MOISÉS** grabs another piña, cuts a chunk out, bites.)*

This one's a little shy...

> *[She continues to flicker.]*

She'll take some patience to bring out her sweeter side...

> *(He tosses it aside, picks up another piña, cuts out a piece, bites. She makes a face.)*

Muy mercurial
she'll take a tougher tongue

to tame her...

> [**BELÉN** *flickers faster.*]

> (*He tosses the piña aside, picks another, cuts, bites.*)

¡Uy! A playful piña if I ever tasted one...

> [**BELÉN** *burns bright as she grabs the piña, bites into it.*]

She must've leapt off the branch
so eager she was
to feel the touch
of a tender lip.
Flesh so ripe
hot breath could make her burst
when Plato dreamed of piñas
her image
haunted him in his sleep
made him soak his pillow with saliva...

> (**BELÉN** *tosses the piña high in the air.*)

> (*As* **MOISÉS** *tries desperately to track it,* **BELÉN** *disappears.*)

> (**MOISÉS** *manages to get under the piña, and right as it's about to land in his hands...*)

> (*A knock on the door.*)

> [*The piña instantly turns to sand, which runs through* **MOISÉS**' *outstretched fingers and onto the floor.*]

> (*Another knock.*)

> (**MOISÉS** *wipes the tears from his eyes, approaches* **EUGENIO.**)

> (**MOISÉS** *stares at* **EUGENIO.**)

> (**EUGENIO** *averts his gaze.*)

> (*Silence.*)

MOISÉS. Yes?

EUGENIO. *(A hair too quickly.)* I...realized I forgot to make the second collection on Sunday...

MOISÉS. Not like you.

EUGENIO. *(With a feeble laugh.)* I know, I'm...a little embarrassed to admit it – but I thought I'd ask around, see if anyone would care to contribute...

MOISÉS. I'm afraid I don't have anything for you –

EUGENIO. You haven't...heard what it's for...

> *(**MOISÉS** stares at him. **EUGENIO** clears his throat.)*

The village clinic in Medrano –

MOISÉS. You should probably be on your way, shouldn't you?

So many other doors to knock on, and so little daylight left...

Wouldn't want to have to stumble home in the dark. Risk falling on your face.

> *(Pause.)*

Pues...

> *(**EUGENIO** doesn't move.)*

What right do you have?

EUGENIO. Huh...?

MOISÉS. Inventing some excuse to come knock on my door –

EUGENIO. Excuse? There's no –

MOISÉS. If a man like me decided to drink his life away, I'd say that's his right.

But you? What's your excuse?

EUGENIO. I think you're mistaken. I...haven't been –

MOISÉS. I can smell it.

> *(Silence.)*

Pathetic.

> *(**MOISÉS** turns away.)*

EUGENIO. Please...

MOISÉS. *What?*

EUGENIO. ...

MOISÉS. If this is about the radio –

EUGENIO. It's –

MOISÉS. *(Walking away.)* – Tell Alamar I'll buy another one –

EUGENIO. It's *not*...about the radio.

It's about...about...

MOISÉS. How about you come back when you're sober?

(Continuing to walk away.)

Should buy me a decade...

EUGENIO. I need you to open the clinic.

*(**MOISÉS** freezes.)*

There are two...orphans in the church right now...who –

MOISÉS. *(Almost muttered.)* Take them to Pilar –

EUGENIO. – Six and eight years old – they've come down with some kind of fever and –

MOISÉS. Did you not hear me the first time?

EUGENIO. I already took them.

The Red Cross turned them away.

They're overrun with children who have this same... same...

MOISÉS. What?

EUGENIO. They're not sure – an infection or a fever – it afflicts only children and it's killed...twenty from their count. They've never seen anything like it – the children...have these boils all over their body – these boils that have the strangest smell, almost sweet...

MOISÉS. You think I'm such an idiot that I'll believe the first fool who comes along spinning stories –

EUGENIO. Twenty dead already, and more dying by the hour. Don't do it for me. Do it for them.

MOISÉS. How about I don't do it at all?

EUGENIO. I promise to never knock on your door again.

(**MOISÉS** *looks at him.*)

Will you come? And do what you can? For them?

Six

> (**LUIS**, *asleep in bed.*)
>
> (**MÓNICA** *sits on the ground at the foot of the bed, an ice pack over her eye.*)

MÓNICA. The day they passed the Amnesty?

Is the first time he asks for Ailén by name.

I get home from cleaning my last house, and he's already asleep.

So I do my nightly ritual...

> (**MÓNICA** *stands, faces* **LUIS.**)
>
> [**LUIS** *tosses, turns.*]

I'm writing you a love letter, Luis.

It is the same letter I've written you every day for the last four years.

I'm mixing my sweat and saliva into the ink with which I will write it

putting my pubes into the pulp I will use to make the paper

and scratching the words onto the page with the tips of my overgrown nails.

And when I have finished this letter

when I have sealed the envelope

put the postage on it

I am going to grind it into a fine powder

and stir it into your sopa de tomate

so when you swallow it

it will go straight to your stomach

where they say the heart of a man really resides

and while it's down there

doing the mad dance of your gastric juices

the Pasodoble of your enzymes

the Bachata of your bile

it will find you, Luis

the real you, Luis

the Luis who before leaving home on that fateful day
four years ago

stuck his tongue deep down my throat and said,

"Be back in five weeks, negra."

The Luis who could read my deepest thoughts from the
smell of my sweat

the Luis who was cocky enough to believe we could
conquer the world

and cocky enough to make it happen...

It will find that Luis

and bring him back to me.

And written on this love letter

my love letter

are the same two sentences I've written every day for
the last four years.

"I would've been happy without the washer, Luis. I
would've loved you just the same."

> [**LUIS** *continues to toss.*]

> *(One particularly violent toss wakes him.)*

Another dream?

> *(He looks at her.)*

You were tossing.

LUIS. You were watching?

MÓNICA. *(Removing the ice pack to reveal a black eye.)* You
knocked me off the bed.

> *(No answer.)*

I'll get you some water.

LUIS. Not thirsty.

MÓNICA. A tortilla, then.

LUIS. Mónica –

MÓNICA. What?

LUIS. Ailén's asleep?

> *(Brief pause.)*

MÓNICA. I'll get her.

> (**MÓNICA** *exits, returns with Ailén in her arms.*)

LUIS. Didn't want you to wake her.

MÓNICA. She sleeps in fits and starts. She'll be fine.

> (**LUIS** *looks at his daughter.*)

You should hold her.

LUIS. I...

MÓNICA. Just take her in your arms like this...like soft...like pillows under her head.

LUIS. No puedo.

MÓNICA. Just let her relax into them –

LUIS. I'm too clumsy.

MÓNICA. No, mi vida...

> (*Gently dropping Ailén into his arms.*)

Shhh...there...see? ¿Fácil, no?

LUIS. (*Looking at his daughter.*) This is what we stopped fighting for?

MÓNICA. Yes.

LUIS. So she wouldn't have to see?

> (*She nods.*)
>
> (*Silence.*)
>
> (*He looks at Ailén in his arms.*)

I remember the first time they told us to kill the children. How they told us to do it without wasting any bullets. We were supposed to...hold their forehead in the palm of our hand...and dash the back of their heads against a rock. It was so simple to kill them that way. Their soft heads like little loaves of bread.

> (*His arms tremble.*)
>
> (*Ailén cries.*)
>
> (**MÓNICA** *quickly grabs Ailén and puts her back in the crib.*)

*(She looks at **LUIS**.)*

LUIS. We had to do it.

MÓNICA. Of course.

LUIS. It was all part of the way we... It was all... We had to –

MÓNICA. Shhh...

(She approaches, kisses him softly.)

Shhh...

(She kisses him all over.)

(He doesn't respond to her touch.)

(She takes off his shirt, climbs on top of him, continues kissing him.)

Seven

(**MOISÉS** *and* **EUGENIO** *in the empty space.*)

EUGENIO. I watch Moisés search in vain
for the keys to the clinic
before he picks up
the hammer he used
to smash Alamar's radio...

(**MOISÉS** *grips the hammer in his hand.*)

...and leads me
across la plaza.

[*The* **TOWN** *appears across the space, holding
the clinic door in front of them like a shield.*]

(*The slightly faded palm prints still scar the
face of the door.*)

[*The* **TOWN** *makes the door dance as they inch
the door across the space...*]

[*Until they hold the door right in front of*
MOISÉS *and* **EUGENIO.**]

(**MOISÉS** *stares at the door for a long moment.*)

(*He holds the hammer out for* **EUGENIO**, *turns
his back.*)

[**EUGENIO** *swings the hammer at the lock.*]

(The sound of metal striking metal.)

[*And again.*]

(The sound of the lock breaking.)

TOWN. Moisés steps inside the clinic
for the first time
since that day...

(**MOISÉS** *surveys the operating table, brushes
it clean with his open palm.*)

(*He starts to roll up his sleeves. Slowly,
meticulously.*)

[*As he does, the Sargento's silhouette flickers to life on the scrim behind him.*]

[*The Sargento also meticulously rolls up his sleeves. Perfectly in time with* **MOISÉS**.]

(The sound of running water.)

EUGENIO. I place the eight-year-old on his operating table.

[**MOISÉS** *scrubs his hands. The precision with which he does so is ritualistic.*]

[*As* **MOISÉS** *scrubs...*]

[*We watch the Sargento place a small metal box on a table and plug wires into both ends of it. The Sargento continues to tinker with the box...*]

(*While* **MOISÉS** *approaches the empty operating table.*)

MOISÉS. My name is Moisés. And I'm here to help.
I'll need you to lift your shirt. So I can see.
I know it does. But I'm trying to make it better...

EUGENIO. The boy lifts his shirt
and Moisés examines the boils
making careful note of the color
the shape
texture
and then he...
lightly presses each boil
with the tip of his finger.
But the boy
screams out in pain
stunning Moisés...

[**BELÉN** *appears on an operating table identical to the empty one in front of* **MOISÉS**.]

[**BELÉN** *has wires hooked to the bottoms of her bare feet.*]

[*She opens her mouth to moan in agony, but...*]

(*The scream of a small boy emerges.*)

MOISÉS. (*Steadying himself.*) Close your eyes, hijo.
And count with me to ten.

> (**MOISÉS** *picks up a scalpel off a nearby tray.*)
>
> [*The Sargento hits a button on the metal box, holds the ends of the two wires to each other, watches the sparks jump from one to the other...*]
>
> (*As* **MOISÉS** *holds the scalpel out over the empty operating table, starts to count.*)

Uno...dos...

EUGENIO. But when you ask a boy...

MOISÉS. Tres...

EUGENIO. ...To close his eyes...

MOISÉS. Cuatro...

EUGENIO. ...He's bound to peek
at least once...

MOISÉS. Cinco...

EUGENIO. ...And soon as the boy
sees the scalpel...

> [*The Sargento presses the button on the metal box, holds it down.*]
>
> [**BELÉN**'s *body tenses as the electric shock courses through it.*]
>
> [*Her mouth opens wide, and...*]
>
> (*The scream of a small boy emerges.*)
>
> (**MOISÉS** *panics.*)

MOISÉS. I need you to –

> [*Another shock.* Another scream.]

– stop screaming –

> [*Another shock.* Another scream.]

I can't...concentrate when you're –

> [*Another shock.* Another scream.]

MOISÉS. – When you're –

> *[Another shock. Another scream.]*

Will you SHUT UP?!

> *(The screaming only intensifies.)*
>
> *(**MOISÉS** drops the scalpel, runs out.)*
>
> *[The silhouette vanishes.]*
>
> *(Across the space, the light reveals **MÓNICA** in her home. She holds Ailén, hums a gentle melody. **LUIS** enters.)*

MÓNICA. Where were you?

> *(**LUIS** says nothing.)*

I've been waiting up.

LUIS. I wish you wouldn't.

> *(**MOISÉS** comes across the pile of piñas, which he begins to devour voraciously.)*

MÓNICA. She couldn't sleep.

LUIS. Es una nena. All she does is sleep. You put her in her crib and she sleeps and it's simple –

MÓNICA. She started crying and nothing I could do would stop her.

I picked her up, held her to me. Her forehead was on fire.

And when I took her temperature I saw...

> *(She holds up Ailén.)*
>
> *(We see the boils on Ailén's body.)*
>
> *(Lights fade on **MÓNICA** and **LUIS**.)*
>
> *(**MOISÉS** continues devouring one piña after another, speaking while he does...)*

MOISÉS. Te extraño tanto, Belén
I miss you when I lie awake
tracing your imprint in our sheets
I miss the music in your laugh
every time I tell a joke –

(A knock on the door.)

*(**EUGENIO** appears.)*

EUGENIO. Moisés, you...

MOISÉS. You promised.

EUGENIO. I know, but...but...but –

MOISÉS. *Never again* you said –

EUGENIO. – You'll never...believe it –

MOISÉS. Why can't you understand –

EUGENIO. – Never believe what...what –

MOISÉS. – The more you talk the less I remember what she
smelled like –

EUGENIO. Moisés you have to...to –

MOISÉS. – The more I hear your voice the less I hear hers –

EUGENIO. The boy's healed.

(Silence.)

MOISÉS. He...

EUGENIO. As soon
as you left
the boils
started to shrivel
and shrink –

MOISÉS. But I didn't...*do* anything –

EUGENIO. You healed him.

(Darkness.)

*[The light reveals the **TOWN** around the edges
of the space, each member holding a small
bell.]*

*[One member of the **TOWN** strikes their bell
over and over...]*

As I lead Moisés across la plaza
I feel the weight
of so many stares
and glance about

to see a face
in every window.

> (**EUGENIO** *looks around at the* **TOWN**, *who holds its gaze fixed on him.*)

EUGENIO. I'm not sure Moisés notices.
He's too distracted
by the boy's unblemished body.

> (**MOISÉS** *stares at the empty operating table as* the insistent bell continues to toll.)

I carry in a six-year-old
whose body is riddled with boils...

> (**MOISÉS** *casts an uneasy glance at* **EUGENIO**, *who nods.*)

Moisés presses his palms
to her stomach...

> (**MOISÉS** *holds his hands over the operating table.*)

The boils shrink
into her body
and disappear.

> (The second bell starts to toll.)

MOISÉS. It's not...real. It can't be real...

> (The third bell starts to toll.)

EUGENIO. I thought the same thing. But you can't deny what we just saw –

MOISÉS. Es una mentira. It's a trick. You're tricking me. To get me back in here – you're doing this, aren't you?!

EUGENIO. How could I?

> (**MOISÉS** *is speechless.*)

> (The fourth bell starts to toll.)

> (**MOISÉS** *stares at his open palms.*)

(The bells toll and toll.)

(And as **MOISÉS** *and* **EUGENIO** *vanish…)*

(The sound of the bells is swallowed by the cry of a lone child.)

(In another part of the space, **LUIS** *looks at Ailén, who lies atop his kitchen table.)*

*(***MÓNICA*** enters.* **LUIS** *looks at her.)*

(She picks up Ailén.)

MÓNICA. It started in some villages northwest of here. And swept across the countryside so fast that…

LUIS. What?

MÓNICA. No tiene nombre. They can't even catch up with it enough to name it.

And it's already killed hundreds.

LUIS. How long…does she…

MÓNICA. Two weeks. If we're lucky.

But the doctor said there's a man who's able to cure it.

LUIS. But if no one understands it –

MÓNICA. I don't think he understands it, either. He just…

LUIS. What?

MÓNICA. Heals.

LUIS. Like a…a –

MÓNICA. This man is a doctor, and…they say he was trying to treat this child, and all he did was touch the boy, and they say his touch made the boy whole. No one knows how, but they say he touches the children, and his touch makes them whole.

(Beat.)

We have to take Ailén.

LUIS. Where?

MÓNICA. To this man, Luis. To see if he can heal her.

(The sound of running water.)

[Across the space, **MOISÉS** *scrubs his hands.]*

MÓNICA. In this village called San Isidro. He's been the doctor at the clinic there for years and no one knew he had this power –

LUIS. San Isidro...

> [As **MOISÉS** *continues scrubbing,* we hear a single, hushed prayer.]

MÓNICA. You've heard of it?

LUIS. No. No.

> [*Lights reveal a single member of the* **TOWN**, *keening, praying.*]

MÓNICA. The next bus leaves in an hour.

LUIS. I don't think it's a good idea, Mónica.

MÓNICA. Luis –

LUIS. I know it's not a good idea.

MÓNICA. Then what do you suggest we do?

> [*More and more of the* **TOWN** *enters, swelling into a single mass that keens, prays, breathes as one.*]

LUIS. When people have no hope, they make up anything to believe in.

I've seen the things a dying soldier will do if he thinks it'll buy him an extra hour of life. Watched men turn themselves into animales and it disgusts me, Mónica –

MÓNICA. We have to try.

> (The single hushed prayer has swelled into a mass prayer.)

LUIS. We'll pray. Put our faith in God, instead of some... some –

MÓNICA. And let our daughter die of something that has no name?

> (**MÓNICA** *and* **LUIS** *vanish.*)
>
> [*As* **MOISÉS** *continues scrubbing...*]
>
> (And the mass prayer throbs throughout the space...)

Eight

TOWN. Within a week
    the streets of San Isidro
    choke with pilgrims
        vagabundos
              idle gawkers.
Each night
the church is packed
                twenty-five to a pew.
        You rent space on your floor
        to those who can afford it.
At sunrise
we surround the clinic.
    I shower it
        with prayers
  bendiciones
              incantations
while child
after child
cycles through.

    *[***MOISÉS*** *does the dance of the miracle cure.]*
    (The mass prayer hums behind him.)

EUGENIO. Moisés heals
hundreds of children
and each time
I expect to be disappointed
to be jolted
out of this dream
but he lays his open palm
on every child
makes the boils fizzle
fade
and I am astonished.

TOWN.   He heals
                              round-the-clock
              sleeping only ten minutes
                    at a time
              heals with such dizzying speed

                                   such singular focus
                    it exhausts

                                   me

                         us

                    just to watch...

          *[***MOISÉS*** *dances and dances.]*
          [The **TOWN** *keens and prays.]*
          [Until **MOISÉS** *cries out...]*

MOISÉS. No entiendo...

              (The mass prayer softens. **EUGENIO** *approaches.)*

No entiendo nada...

EUGENIO. We can bring in the Bishop. To investigate. See if
    there's not another explanation.

MOISÉS. If I can keep it up.

EUGENIO. If you need more rest –

MOISÉS. It's not that –

EUGENIO. – I think everyone would understand –

MOISÉS. There's a time
    in the first two years of life
    when a baby's face
    is a perfect reflection
    of its father's...
    I see faces
    and faces
    and faces
    in front of me
    faces I think I must recognize
    and I can't help but wonder...

Where are the fathers?
Dead and in the ground?
Waiting at home?
Outside my door?

> *(Beat.)*

Why me?
Why is this happening to me?

EUGENIO. Don't question it, Moisés.

MOISÉS. How can I not?

EUGENIO. It is a gift.

MOISÉS. There is no such thing.

> (**MOISÉS** *turns back to the operating table.*)
>
> (**MÓNICA** *enters another part of the space.*)

MÓNICA. I leave Luis behind
and catch the first bus
to San Isidro.

> *(A small bundle appears in front of* **MOISÉS**
> *on the operating table.*)
>
> *(It's a baby girl.)*

Eight hours we wait in line
watching every child
come out of the clinic
healthy, healed...

MOISÉS. *(Looking at the child.)* She's young.

MÓNICA. ...Eight hours
until the priest
takes Ailén
out of my arms...

EUGENIO. Three months.

MÓNICA. ...And tells me to wait
outside the open clinic door.

MOISÉS. Where's she from?

EUGENIO. Ojona.

(**MOISÉS** *opens the bundle, staggers back, momentarily stunned.*)

EUGENIO. Are you alright...?

MOISÉS. Her face...looks so...

EUGENIO. Is something wrong with her –

MOISÉS. It's...so...

EUGENIO. What?

(**MOISÉS** *peers at the child, staggers back again.*)

Moisés...?

[We see a hazy silhouette materialize on the scrim behind them.]

MOISÉS. What's her name?

EUGENIO. *(Consulting his list.)* It says right here –

MOISÉS. Last name.

Her last name

is all I want to

need to –

EUGENIO. Saavedra.

[The silhouette comes fully into focus.]

[It is the Sargento's.]

(**MOISÉS** *and* **EUGENIO** *look at each other.*)

EUGENIO & MOISÉS. Sargento...

TOWN. A moment later

the healer stumbles out of the clinic...

(**MOISÉS** *stumbles into the empty space.*)

...Slams the door behind him...

[The **TOWN** *pulls the clinic door out from the middle of its single, keening mass and thrusts it into the light.]*

...and on the outside of it...

[We see the smattering of white palm prints on it.]

> *[The print in the middle of the door shimmers, burns bright.]*
>
> *[This print is missing the top half of its ring finger.]*

MÓNICA. ...I see my husband's hand.

> *(Silence.)*
>
> *(The scrim falls to the floor with a thunderous sound.)*
>
> *(Behind it, we see* **LUIS** *in his army fatigues.)*
>
> *(***MÓNICA*** stares at her husband, astonished. She reaches out, tries to touch him but is unable to, as he continues past her toward the center of the space.)*
>
> *(***BELÉN***'s body appears in front of* **MOISÉS***.)*
>
> *(***MOISÉS*** kneels before her.)*

LUIS. We need your help, doctór.

MOISÉS. My...?

LUIS. You left us no choice. We caught the two of you holding that guerrillero *in your arms* outside that church and...we just had to hook her up to that car battery, had to keep giving it to her and giving it to her, make sure she never does it again –

MOISÉS. I don't understand what you want me to –

LUIS. *(Tossing* **MOISÉS** *a defibrillator.)* Shock her back to life.

> *(***MOISÉS*** stares at* **BELÉN***.)*

Your wife, tu santuario, the love of your life lies before you, and you have the power to re-write this story, to take her home and live out the rest of your days – isn't that what you want?

> *(***MOISÉS*** picks up the defibrillator, presses the handles together, puts them on* **BELÉN***'s chest.)*
>
> *(Nothing.)*

Come on come on come on come on –

(Tries again.)

(Still nothing.)

LUIS. Come *on* –

(A third time.)

(**BELÉN** *opens her eyes.*)

We all stand in the street...

EUGENIO. Watching while Moisés...

MÓNICA. Talks to himself.

MOISÉS. She's...she's...

LUIS. I knew it! *Knew* those healing hands wouldn't fail us. If you could bring back that son of a bitch who killed my men... We drove that hijo de puta to the edge of death, left him lying there, but you – no sé como lo hiciste – you pulled him off that precipice, and I just *knew* you could do it again –

BELÉN. *(A whisper to* **MOISÉS.**) Why...?

LUIS. *(Calling offstage.)* ¡Felipe! ¡Nesto! Get the truck going! We're taking her with us!

BELÉN. *Why...?*

MOISÉS. But you...you said I could –

LUIS. I lied.

(Calling off.)

¡Ahora!

(**LUIS** *grabs hold of* **BELÉN** *to drag her off.*)

MOISÉS. Take me. I'm asking you, begging you, to take *me*, leave her behind –

LUIS. *(With a laugh.)* Why on earth would I –

MOISÉS. *I'm* the one who healed him, the one who flaunted it in your face – you're supposed to punish *me*...

LUIS. I am, amigo.

You've got a long, long life ahead of you.

(**LUIS** *kicks* **MOISÉS.**)

(**MOISÉS** *falls to the ground in agony, releasing* **LUIS**' *leg.*)

(**LUIS** *drags* **BELÉN** *offstage, leaving a bright red streak of blood behind her.*)

(*All the while we hear her whispers...*)

BELÉN. *Why...? Why...? Why...?*

(**MOISÉS** *reaches out desperately, tries to grab* **BELÉN**.)

BELÉN & MOISÉS. *Why...?*

(**LUIS** *and* **BELÉN** *disappear.*)

(**MOISÉS** *comes to, sees everybody watching him.*)

(*He looks at* **MÓNICA**...*Ailén...then back to* **MÓNICA**...)

MOISÉS. Yours?

(**MÓNICA** *picks up the child...*)

MÓNICA. Her name's Ailén.

MOISÉS. Beautiful name.

MÓNICA. Thank you.

MOISÉS. Never got to name mine.

(*Long silence.*)

MÓNICA. I... I am...

MOISÉS. Don't say it all at once.

MÓNICA. I'm...

MOISÉS. Sorry?

(*She nods.*)

How sorry?

MÓNICA. No hay palabras.

MOISÉS. Try

MÓNICA. ...

MOISÉS. Try harder.

MÓNICA. Tell me how.

MOISÉS. Try him in your heart. Convict him there. Once you've done that simple, simple thing no one has dared to, walk out on him. Promise he'll never see her again.

   (Silence.)

Not sorry enough.

   (He starts offstage.)

MÓNICA. She has nothing to do with this.

MOISÉS. She has everything to do with it.

MÓNICA. She wasn't even born when it happened.

MOISÉS. He came back from the war, you knew the things he'd done, the person he was –

MÓNICA. The things, yes, but not the person –

MOISÉS. You still let him *penetrarte*, let his urchin fester for *nine months*! –

MÓNICA. I thought she'd...bring him back to me.

   *(**MOISÉS** laughs.)*

I thought she'd...that he'd see her and she'd crack through...whatever it is the war put between us, and kill the man who did those things...

MOISÉS. Do you still? Believe that can happen?

MÓNICA. I don't know. I don't know I don't know I don't know...

All I know is...there would be weeks on end when he wouldn't say a word to me. Wouldn't even look me in the eye, so I'd...wait till he was asleep. Till he was doing his nightly dance with violent dreams. That's when I'd climb on top of him, while he clawed at me. Battered away till I bled. Por tres meses – ninety fucking days – I made him paint my body with scars, made him bore a hole through me until... Ailén.

I am...*so* sorry for your loss, no hay palabras, pero...if you take my baby girl from me...

MOISÉS. Bring him here. Make him ask me.

(Beat.)

MÓNICA. Thank you so –

MOISÉS. Not yet.

> *(She looks at **MOISÉS** for a moment.)*
>
> *(She leaves Ailén on the operating table, runs offstage.)*
>
> *(**MOISÉS** looks at the child.)*

Nine

*(**LUIS** at the kitchen table.)*

LUIS. *(Staring into space.)* I've been waiting for you. Soon as you left, I sat here, and...started to pray. To try to... wash away her boils with my words, make a miracle of my own, so you wouldn't have to take her. I started to say the Our Father, but I...can't seem to remember how it goes... So glad you're here. So glad you're back. To help me remember. Padre Nuestro... Padre Nuestro...

MÓNICA. You knew.

LUIS. I said I don't know the words –

MÓNICA. You. Knew.

(He looks up at her.)

LUIS. Where's Ailén?

MÓNICA. The children went in there sick and suffering, and when they came out...it was the most amazing thing I've ever seen –

LUIS. Where is Ailén?

MÓNICA. On his table. Waiting for him to heal her.

LUIS. Then he's going to...

MÓNICA. You tell me.

He's waiting for you to go ask him.

(Silence.)

LUIS. His hands, Mónica...when they touch her, he will get inside her –

MÓNICA. I don't care, Luis –

LUIS. This is a man who helped heal guerrilleros –

MÓNICA. I don't care what he did –

LUIS. Who brought them back to life so they could turn my men to dust –

MÓNICA. I don't care if he helped kill a hundred thousand soldados or how proud you are of what you did to him, you will go there and beg him for forgiveness if that's what it takes. He has our daughter. And if you love her –

LUIS. I *do* –

MÓNICA. If you care one bit about her –

LUIS. But I can stay right here and make my own miracle –

MÓNICA. *Luis* –

LUIS. I can!

 (Silence.)

 If you'll just...if you'll help me remember... Padre Nuestro... Padre Padre Padre Nuestro...

MÓNICA. Four years I've stood here in this house and played the dutiful soldier's wife.

LUIS. Padre Padre Padre Padre –

MÓNICA. Did everything you told me. Asked no questions while you went out to kill and kill and kill –

LUIS. Padre Padre –

MÓNICA. While the man I married, while mi amor slipped away. And all the life drained out of him –

LUIS. Padre –

MÓNICA. Did I say something? No. I obeyed. I lost friends and family, my own mother won't talk to me because of the things you did. Did I question you? No. I obeyed. I will not obey anymore. So if you are too much of a coward...

LUIS. I am not –

MÓNICA. If you are too much of a *cobarde* to go ask him – if you let my daughter *die*... I will leave you, Luis. I will take Ailén with me, claw deep down into the dirt con estas garras, put her somewhere you will never find her, and I will leave this place and never come back so help me God...

LUIS. You wouldn't...

MÓNICA. If you let my daughter die.

Ten

(Lights reveal Ailén lying on a separate table.)

*[**MOISÉS** does the dance of the miracle cure before the empty operating table.]*

TOWN. Moisés begins healing again
and the crowds
trickle back.

*[The **TOWN** lumbers on in a line that resembles a chain gang more than anything else.]*

We try
to praise the greatness
of the man among us
try to thank El Señor
for his wondrous gift
but every sign of the cross
every joyous shout
or uttered prayer
feels flimsy
hollow.
So one by one
we stop
and wait our turn
eyes straight ahead
like we're in line
at the post office.

EUGENIO. Then I see
commotion
at the edge of the crowd...

*[The **TOWN** collapses back into a single, throbbing mass.]*

...and I know...

(**MÓNICA** *addresses the audience.*)

MÓNICA. Soon as we step off the bus
I feel everyone's gaze fixed on us...

EUGENIO. My breath shortens
at the thought
of seeing him again...

MÓNICA. But I keep my eyes
straight ahead
as we ride a wave of whispers
into town...

> [*The* **TOWN** begins showering the space with
> wave after wave of indecipherable whispers
> *as they part...*]

> (*And reveal* **LUIS** *standing behind them.*)

EUGENIO. He's so much smaller
than I remembered
and his face
is a mask
two sizes too big.

> [*The* **TOWN** continues showering the space
> with whispers *as they fan out to the edges of
> the space.*]

LUIS. Moisés!

EUGENIO & TOWN. Will Moisés see
the same man I do?

LUIS. Moisés!

EUGENIO & TOWN. Or will his rage
make this broken man
ten meters tall?
Give him
sharp
eager eyes?

LUIS. MOISÉS!

(Inside the clinic, **MOISÉS** *lays his hand on his scalpel.)*

EUGENIO & TOWN. Erase his wrinkles?
Smooth his scars?

*(***MOISÉS*** decides to leave the scalpel lying where it is.)*

LUIS. *(Howling.)* MOISÉS!

MOISÉS. *(Stepping into the center of the space.)* I'm here.

(Silence.)

LUIS. You're not the only one, you know. Who's making miracles.
This other doctor discovered he has the power. Just like you. He'd been working in this village for years and no one knew. Then it just happened. The other day. He started healing people. Not far from here.

MOISÉS. Isn't that extraordinary.

LUIS. Miracles happening all over.

MOISÉS. What's his name?

LUIS. I... You know, I can't remember.

MOISÉS. Shame.

LUIS. *(With a feeble laugh.)* The funniest thing. That I can't remember.

MOISÉS. Not far from here.

LUIS. Why I came. To tell you.

MOISÉS. That's great.

LUIS. Yeah.

MOISÉS. Convenient.

LUIS. Thought so, too.

MOISÉS. You should take your daughter to him.

*(***LUIS*** does nothing.)*

(Ailén lightly cries.)

*(***LUIS*** tries to hide its effect on him.)*

Or say what it is you really came to say.

LUIS. Don't know what you're talking about –

MOISÉS. "I need your help."

> *(Silence.)*

Simple, simple words.

LUIS. I...

MOISÉS. Yes?

LUIS. I... I...can't.

> *(Beat.)*

I don't believe it.

MOISÉS. What's there not to believe? Your daughter is dying. That is *a fact*. The moon orbits the earth. The earth orbits the sun. Your daughter is dying. And only I can heal her.

LUIS. ...

MOISÉS. Do you want your daughter to die?

LUIS. She's not...

MOISÉS. Do you want your daughter to die?

LUIS. *No.*

MOISÉS. Pues dímelo.

LUIS. He...heh...help me.

MOISÉS. What?

LUIS. Help me. I want you to help me.

MOISÉS. No No *No.*

LUIS. You said –

MOISÉS. *Need.* I said neeeeeed. Say it with me. Neeeeeeeed.

LUIS. But I –

MOISÉS. Just words. Worthless little words.

LUIS. Then why do you want them?

MOISÉS. I'm poor. I don't have the words you have. I don't get to say wife. Or daughter.

> *(Ailén cries louder.)*

> *(Tears stream down **LUIS**' face.)*

LUIS. What do words matter when you have my tears?

MOISÉS. If I want both? Who are you to say no?

    (Beat.)

LUIS. I...

MOISÉS. Yes?

LUIS. ...Need your help. I need your help.

    (MOISÉS *nods slightly to himself.)*

    (Brief pause.)

MOISÉS. "And I am a murderer."

LUIS. But –

MOISÉS. Go ahead.

LUIS. I am a...a...

MOISÉS. *Mur*der –

LUIS. I am a murderer.

MOISÉS. "And I deserve to die."

LUIS. And I deserve to die.

MOISÉS. Feel free to beg.

    (No answer.)

Whenever you're ready.

LUIS. *(Slowly dropping to his knees.)* Please...please forgive me, I...want you to forgive I need you to forgive me –

MOISÉS. Beg me. *Me.* My name is Moisés.

LUIS. Please, Moisés, I am nothing and you are everything and I am a murderer un asesino un hijo de puta so please forgive me, Moisés. I beg you for forgiveness, Moisés, beg you to heal my...my...

MOISÉS. Thank you.

That's what I needed to hear.

Don't forget to take your daughter with you.

    (MOISÉS *doesn't move.)*

LUIS. But you didn't...do anything...

MOISÉS. I said you're free to go.

LUIS. You promised you would –

MOISÉS. I lied.

(**LUIS** *just stares at* **MOISÉS**.)

Pues lárgate.

LUIS. You...hijo de puta... I'm going to –

MOISÉS. Nothing.

You're going to pick her up, walk away, and I will never see you again.

(**LUIS** *does nothing.*)

(Ailén *continues to cry.*)

What are you waiting for? Pick her up and –

LUIS. I...can't.

MÓNICA. (*Stepping into the scene.*) He...

LUIS. Her head. In my hands.

MOISÉS. What are you –

LUIS. Will crumble. And I can't...

(*Silence.*)

(**MOISÉS** *looks at* **MÓNICA** *and* **EUGENIO**, *who stand there, watching.*)

MOISÉS. Will someone take this child off my table?!

(*No one moves.*)

(**MOISÉS** *starts off.*)

EUGENIO. (*Blurting out.*) But...

(**MOISÉS** *stops, turns to* **EUGENIO**.)

...but...

MOISÉS. Now he speaks.

EUGENIO. ...

MOISÉS. Go back to nursing your flask.

EUGENIO. You're going to leave her lying there?

MOISÉS. I learned from the best.

EUGENIO. It won't bring her back...

MOISÉS. Lástima. I was under the impression it would.

EUGENIO. Or dull the pain...

MOISÉS. Feels pretty fucking good right now.

(**MOISÉS** *keeps walking.*)

EUGENIO. You're a selfish fucking *bastard*!

(**MOISÉS** *stops, stares at* **EUGENIO.**)

A selfish, *selfish* man who can't even look up from his navel long enough to see how many people would kill for the gift you have. *Kill* to be able to reach out, touch something – someone – and erase all the...the...the...

MOISÉS. You were born a coward, you've lived your life like one, and that's how you'll die.

EUGENIO. Moisés –

MOISÉS. And nothing you do
will ever make up
for how you failed us –

EUGENIO. What would Belén think of –

(**MOISÉS** *violently grabs* **EUGENIO.**)

MOISÉS. Do you really think
your little lips
are worthy
of uttering her name?

EUGENIO. But –

MOISÉS. *(Tightening his grip.)* Anything you say
or do
any *attempt*
to atone
insults her *memory*...

(*A subtle, but palpable, break.*)

(**MOISÉS** *lets go of* **EUGENIO.**)

(**MÓNICA** *steps forward.*)

MÓNICA. What if...I promise to keep your wife's memory alive?

MOISÉS. How could you?

MÓNICA. I could...tell Ailén what my husband did. Who he did it to.

MOISÉS. You wouldn't.

MÓNICA. I will.

LUIS. Mónica...

MOISÉS. You're lying.

MÓNICA. If that's what it takes.

LUIS. Pero...

MÓNICA. I'll whisper it in her ear every day. Make sure she never forgets.

LUIS. Pero pero...

MOISÉS. She'll blame you, too. Just as much as she'll blame him.

MÓNICA. She will.

MOISÉS. And grow up to resent you –

LUIS. Mónica –

MOISÉS. Barely stand the sight of you –

MÓNICA. But she'll be alive.

> *(Pause.)*

MOISÉS. Bring her to me.

> *(***EUGENIO*** rushes to the table, picks up Ailén.)*

LUIS. *(To* **MÓNICA.***)* Pero qué...qué has hecho...?

> *(***EUGENIO*** hands the child to* **MOISÉS.***)*

> *[***MOISÉS*** holds her up.]*

MOISÉS. *(To* **LUIS.***)* May she live
a long
long life
full of resentment
for the things
you did.
May she never
look at you
without seeing
the faces
of your victims

in the black
of your eyes...

    *(**MOISÉS** places Ailén in **LUIS**' arms.)*

    [Both their hands are on Ailén at once.]

TOWN. When both their hands
are on the child
someone shouts
Look up!
and there are
spots on the sun
seven spots
that writhe
and dance
before our eyes
as every child is healed...

    *(**MOISÉS** leaves Ailén in **LUIS**' hands.)*

And when the healer
takes his hands off the child
there is a patch
of bright white skin
in the shape of his hand
emblazoned on her belly.

    *(**LUIS** holds Ailén in his arms.)*

    [The white palm print burns bright on her stomach.]

    *(**MOISÉS** starts offstage.)*

Then the healer
walks and walks
away...

    *(**MOISÉS** exits.)*

    [His silhouette appears on the scrim.]

[It shrinks and shrinks into a tiny speck.]

[It disappears.]

EUGENIO. No one's seen him since.

MÓNICA. *(Taking the baby out of her husband's arms.)*
Luis, Ailén, and I board the first bus back to Ojona.
And I keep my promise.

> *(She quietly whispers something in Ailén's ear.)*

Remind her how she got her mark.

> *(She lightly kisses the print on Ailén's stomach.)*

But Luis...hasn't said a word since.

> *(***LUIS*** *sits on the floor, staring straight ahead, motionless.)*

He sits in front of the washer all day.

Staring at it.

Sometimes

I see his eyes

move in small circles

willing it

to work.

> *(***MÓNICA***, Ailén, and* ***LUIS*** *vanish.)*

TOWN. Moisés seems to have taken the plague with him.
There have been no new cases since he left.

> But we wait in fear of the day it might return...

EUGENIO. Dreading what we'll do without him.

TOWN. The pilgrims

for their part

have stayed

breathing new life into San Isidro.

> *[The* ***TOWN*** *converges into a single mass that keens, prays, breathes as one.]*

EUGENIO. The Bishop
　　has told me
　　to tear down the clinic
　　and build a shrine
　　in its place.

> *[The* **TOWN** *pulls the clinic door out from itself, thrusts it into the light.]*

> (**EUGENIO** *looks at the palm prints on the door.)*

I'm not sure I should.

> *[The palm prints on the door burn bright.]*

End of Play